Incredibly Insane Sports

FREE RUNNING

By Jessica Cohn

 Gareth Stevens
Publishing

Please visit our website, www.garethstevens.com. For a free color catalog of all our high-quality books, call toll free 1-800-542-2595 or fax 1-877-542-2596.

Library of Congress Cataloging-in-Publication Data

Cohn, Jessica.

 Free running / Jessica Cohn.

    p. cm. — (Incredibly insane sports)

ISBN 978-1-4339-8827-1 (pbk.)

ISBN 978-1-4339-8828-8 (6-pack)

ISBN 978-1-4339-8826-4 (library binding)

1. Running—Juvenile literature. 2. Parkour—Juvenile literature. I. Title.

 GV1061.C63 2013

 796.42—dc23

                        2012037754

First Edition
Published in 2013 by
Gareth Stevens Publishing
111 East 14th Street, Suite 349
New York, NY 10003

©2013 Gareth Stevens Publishing

Produced by Netscribes Inc.
Art Director Dibakar Acharjee
Editorial Content The Wordbench
Copy Editor Sarah Chassé
Picture Researcher Sandeep Kumar G
Designer Rishi Raj
Illustrators Ashish Tanwar, Indranil Ganguly, Prithwiraj Samat, and Rohit Sharma

Photo credits:
Page no. = #, t = top, a = above, b = below, l = left, r = right, c = center
Front Cover: Shutterstock Images LLC Title Page: Shutterstock Images LLC
Contents Page: Shutterstock Images LLC Inside: Shutterstock Images LLC: 4, 5, 6, 7t, 7b, 8, 9t, 9b, 10, 11, 12, 13, 14, 15, 16, 17, 18, 19, 20, 21, 22, 23t, 23b, 24t, 24b, 25, 26, 27, 28, 29, 30, 31, 32, 33, 34, 35, 36, 37, 38, 39, 40, 41, 42,43, 45.

Printed in the United States of America

CPSIA compliance information: Batch #CW13GS: For further information contact Gareth Stevens, New York, New York at 1-800-542-2595.

Contents

ON THE RUN

A free runner sees stairways and bridges as athletic challenges. Railings are objects to jump over. Roofs and walls are surfaces to run across. The world's top free runners can make amazing **freestyle** moves. They can **vault** over moving vehicles. They can leap across rooftops and flip backward from fire escapes. The best among them find ways to make dangerous stunts look easy.

Free running is related to *parkour*, which was started in Europe. *Parkour* is taken from a French term. It comes from *parcours du combattant,* which is a kind of military training.

Mixing It Up

This extreme sport combines running with **gymnastics**. The athletes use the outside world as an open gym. As they run, they use the objects they come across as gym equipment. Each time the runners flip over park benches and roll to their feet, they fine-tune their sense of balance. They learn to flow with their motions.

The rules in free running are few. A free runner chooses the movements he or she will make while running.

5

Free to Be

The idea behind free running is to start moving and not stop, no matter what gets in the way. Each stair or fence in the runner's path becomes part of the running course. In this sport, there is no need to buy expensive equipment. It all starts with a pair of running shoes and a place to run.

To cut down on the chance of injury, runners learn to land on the ball of the foot, rather than the heel.

Jumping In

While in motion, free runners make the effort to show some style. The athletes try to stay moving, making jumps as needed and spins when spinning feels right to the runner. With time, the runners' movements become more graceful. Parks and playgrounds are especially good areas to practice these skills. In spaces set aside for sport, an athlete can more easily move without bothering other people.

Some of the people who have practiced free running a very long time are able to complete long-distance landings.

TEST IT!

Your weight is a measure of Earth's **gravity** pulling on your **mass**. When you run, Earth pulls at you, and your feet push back with similar force. These forces register between your feet and the surface you run on. A free runner learns to throw body weight forward, so less of these forces register. Test how this works by jumping on flat feet from a bottom stair. Then, hop on the bottom stair and off again while moving. Hopping while already in movement feels lighter.

Free for All

In gyms, athletes lift weights and exercise on equipment that builds their strength. In most sports, a special environment is created to test the athletes' skills. Coaches come up with plans to direct the athletes' development. But in free running, nearly the opposite is true. The runners do not often prepare for big events. They let ordinary objects test their skills, and they take whatever comes as a challenge.

The best free runners mix the art of movement and science of motion in everything they do.

Bold and Basic

Free runners say they like the freedom built into the sport, and they feel free to move at their own pace. Most of these athletes are not rushing to be something they are not. They know that skills come with practice, and practice takes time. The runners start by learning some basic moves, such as how to roll, how to land, and how to stay balanced. To avoid injury, they do not push too far too fast.

Competing with other runners is not central to this sport. Free runners run to improve themselves.

TEST IT!

Grab chalk, paper, a tape measure, and a pencil to measure the height of your **vertical** jump.

1. Stand next to a wall and reach as high as possible. Mark the top with chalk.
2. Next, jump from a standing position and touch the wall. Mark where you touched.
3. Measure the distance between the two marks.
4. Practice jumping to make the distance longer.

If 1 inch equals 2.54 centimeters, how many centimeters high is your jump?

Answer: To find the answer, take the number of inches and multiply by 2.54 centimeters.

BEYOND THESE WALLS

The ideas behind free running have long been used to train soldiers. When training for battle, soldiers run through courses that have been set up for them. The courses include ditches and other constructions they might come across in battle.

Overcoming It All

Running through **obstacle** courses helps the soldiers feel ready for anything. In the same way, free runners learn to look at the things around them as obstacles to overcome. This way of seeing the world trains both the body and mind to be stronger.

A free runner keeps his or her mind in gear because successful moves must be sized up in the seconds leading up to them.

On the Go

One of the tricks the runners must learn is staying aware of their surroundings while in movement. The runners have to show respect for others if they want to continue their training. This means getting exercise without getting in the way of other people in the area. It means making sure the coast is clear. There are laws for public spaces, and the athletes do not want to run into trouble with the law.

Free runners take pride in being graceful as they move.

Jump on History

Free running is related to parkour, which was introduced to French soldiers in the early 1900s. The French soldiers were trained on obstacle courses to get them ready for battle. Many people think of free running as the American parkour. But both sports have roots in the **martial arts** of ancient Asia. All of these schools of thought are related, and each can be tied to movie history. The people who do movie stunts use many of the same skills.

An efficient movement is one that does not waste energy. Making efficient moves is key to the practice of parkour.

History in the Making

1920s The French military introduced parkour as part of its training.

1920s Actors such as Buster Keaton performed parkour-like stunts in early films.

1980s An accomplished French runner named David Belle developed parkour as an everyday sport, with the help of some friends.

2000s Belle introduced parkour to wider audiences through music videos and movies.

2006 The James Bond movie *Casino Royale* featured actors with parkour and free running skills.

2012 Parkour professionals were featured in events leading up to the Summer Olympics in London, as well as in related videos.

Free running is a combination of martial arts, the stunts performed in movies, and the freestyle movements of today's extreme sports.

Nature Made

The inventor of parkour was Georges Hébert, who was born in France in 1875. While traveling, he noticed that **indigenous** people who lived in nature were better athletes than those who lived in towns. Hébert taught physical education. He took his thoughts about nature and used them to help train others. "The final goal of physical education is to make strong beings," he said.

Each obstacle requires a different set of responses and actions.

Find and Conquer

Hébert called his ideas the Natural Method. But in this kind of training it is not just natural objects that are used to help people grow stronger. One minute, the runner may swing from branches on a tree. In the next moment, the runner may jump over a park bench. The idea is to do what comes naturally, using different parts of the body. Hébert said people should be "able to walk, run, jump, move on all fours, to climb, to keep balance, to throw, lift, defend [themselves] and to swim."

The playground equipment found in public parks is often built like an obstacle course. Normal outdoor play for children is like free running practice in a number of ways.

TEST IT!

Free runners try to keep up their **momentum**. Sometimes, it can make sense to form the body into rounded shapes for this purpose. To see how, imagine you are a soldier and must stay near the ground to stay safe. First, try crawling on the floor. Then, try rolling like a log to increase your momentum. You can also go outside and try crawling and rolling down a hill. Feel the difference that the hill makes.

EXTREME MEASURES

In London, a 14-year-old recently fell from a roof while trying to jump between two buildings. He was following a friend who made the jump safely. Did he slip? Was he trying too hard to measure up? Each time there is a news report about a runner who is hurt by a stunt, the people who see the story want to know why the runner did not know better.

Risk Management

Free running was an underground activity for many years, but no longer. As the sport grows in popularity, so do the numbers of people who jump in and take risks. Though athletes are expected to take small risks to develop their skills, taking huge risks can ruin the sport for everyone.

Free running can be like an extreme game of follow the leader.

Pride in Safety

One of the first rules of free running is to be true to oneself. New runners need to take it easy and leave leaping over roofs to people who have put in many hours of practice. One wrong move, and the fun turns to danger. A sport like this is dangerous when the participants do not fully understand the risks involved.

In the Area

Free running is also known as **urban** running because cities are often used as training grounds. The city runners jump over objects in parks. They move across streets filled with vehicles. It is very important for the athletes to study their surroundings to stay safe.

A runner needs to keep in mind that not everything is safe to lean on or jump over. Not every bench is bolted to the ground. The best objects to use for practice are those that are secured in place. Otherwise, the object might fall over and break, and the runner might be hurt.

An abandoned building poses far too many risks to be used for free running.

Running with Abandon

Some runners explore construction sites because they do not know better. They run though empty buildings because there is so much space and no one to bother. But they may learn the hard way that even abandoned property belongs to somebody.

New runners need to stick to public places. Otherwise, they can be arrested for being where they do not belong. Running in these areas is also dangerous because they are empty. In a place that has no people, it is harder to get help if someone is hurt.

In some towns where free runners have been reckless, officials have made laws to make the sport illegal.

Comfort Zone

This sport is based on running. But the runners are not in a race. The trickier moves include learning to **scale** walls, and these skills cannot be rushed. When people are ready, they know it, because they have been building up to it. As the athletes practice, they become comfortable with their skills and sure of their movements.

Part of the challenge of free running is being both responsible and creative while on the move.

What Do You Think?

Free running is free of many rules found in regular sports. Yet free runners practice in shared spaces. In what ways do the runners need to follow rules anyway?

The key to excellence in free running is repetition. That is the act of repeating a movement over and over until the body really "knows" it.

Safe and Sound

Safety is always on their minds, whether the runners are thinking about it or not. As free runners practice, they are also working out their minds. The work that they do helps them become more aware of the ways the body and mind work together. The athletes learn to listen to themselves in order to understand what can and cannot be done.

ROLL WITH IT

When done right, free running can be as safe as many other sports, with payoffs that can last much longer. Free running builds the runners' confidence by showing them that they have the strength to meet sudden challenges. This exciting sport is free of gear, and that fact alone is freeing. The athletes realize they do not need much to improve themselves besides a decent pair of shoes.

Some shoe companies are making special free running shoes, in response to the growing popularity of the sport.

If the Shoe Fits
Consider the following when it comes to shoes:

feature	reason
good grip	worn bottoms can lead to accidents
snug fit	loose shoes can lead to trips
thinner sole	thick soles can lead to slipping
short and flat laces	long laces can get caught on obstacles

Get Comfortable

If there is anything the runner needs, it is shoes that fit. When running, the heel hits the ground first. The foot rolls forward on the outside edge. The weight moves to the ball of the foot and then the toes. The big toe does most of the pushing back. Good shoes work with a foot instead of against it.

For safety, the runner's clothes should not be too loose. If they are, they can catch on the obstacles. For comfort, clothing should not be too tight, either. A cap or band can hold long hair in place, and gloves with grips can protect the hands. But the gloves must fit well to be useful. Wearing socks above the anklebones is also recommended because the socks protect the ankles from scrapes.

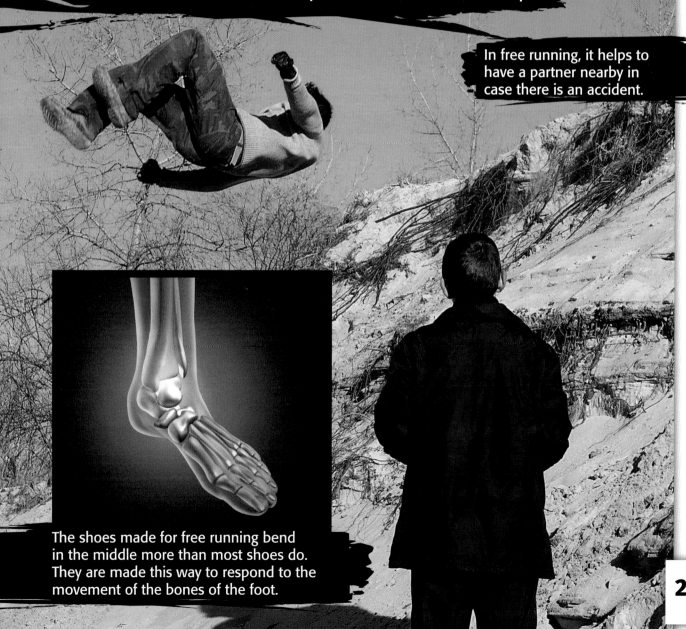

In free running, it helps to have a partner nearby in case there is an accident.

The shoes made for free running bend in the middle more than most shoes do. They are made this way to respond to the movement of the bones of the foot.

23

Measuring Up

To begin training, most free runners simply start to run. They choose a day to go out by themselves or with a partner. New runners have to build their skills in a natural way. The time spent outside gets longer as the athletes grow stronger.

It helps to go outside with a sense of adventure. The first obstacles that most runners try to jump over are low railings and low benches. The idea is to learn to vault the body over the objects without slipping or getting hurt. Each time the runners go out, they can discover new things about themselves and the area where they practice.

Eating right is always important. Drinking enough water is especially important when it is hot outside.

Running Water

Feeling fit and having **stamina** help athletes perform better. To build both, many runners do other exercises when not outside practicing. The chin-ups and crunches done at home will help when out in the field. It also helps to have a healthy diet. This means eating plenty of vegetables, whole grains, fruit, and **protein** without a lot of fat. It means staying **hydrated** and drinking water rather than soft drinks.

Crunches build strength in the abdomen. That is the part of the body between the hips and the chest.

JOINING THE CLUB

It is natural for people to share ideas and interests, so many runners end up looking for clubs they can join. In some cities, there are large clubs that have their own buildings. But most free running groups are people who meet in parks and other places.

Ask to Join

The people who have been free running the longest know the best places to train. Finding a group to join and learn from can be as simple as asking around. But new free runners should beware. The people who run the group should be concerned about the safety of new members. Younger free runners should get the proper permission to join.

Runners should keep repeating the moves long after the skills were mastered the first time.

Drills and Thrills

In some cities, the runners gather in parks to practice drills. They support one another by working side by side. Besides basic push-ups, they perform handstands, cartwheels, and other movements to help bring the body into balance. For some free runners, all they need is a goal and the time to work on it alone. For many others, the support of a group helps keep them on track.

TEST IT!

The pendulum on a grandfather clock is the part that swings back and forth. Its swinging moves the clockwork. To fix a grandfather clock that is running too slowly, someone has to adjust the length of the pendulum. Why? Its speed has to do with its length. There is a law of science called the law of the pendulum. The longer

the pendulum, the more slowly it swings. The same can be said of your arms and legs. To get them to swing faster when you run, you need to shorten them. When a coach tells you to bend your arms, this is why. Bending makes the run more efficient. Try testing this outside by running with your arms straight and then with them bent.

When runners have good form, they swing their arms but do not move their shoulders much.

27

For the Win

Free runners may challenge each other, and even tease one another, but that is often where competition ends. To be a winner in free running, the runner needs to beat his or her own best performance. A runner's friends may weigh in with their opinions. But it is the performer who ultimately judges the performance.

Consider all the things that could be wrong with this picture. Whose property is this? Does the runner know what he is doing?

Adding Up the Answers

Though there are no set rules for this sport, there are questions that a free runner can ask himself or herself.

Is this legal?

Free running is not legal on private property unless the runner has an owner's permission. Using abandoned buildings is usually not legal. Permission must be granted by someone in charge. A building and even an empty area almost always belong to someone.

Is this safe?

The movements look so easy when they are done in movies. But the truth is that free running takes practice. In general, showing off is not safe.

How can I improve this?

A runner can improve his or her moves with practice. There is no way to get around the need to repeat the moves until they become second nature. Setting goals and reaching them in this sport takes time and willpower.

In Training

In the city of Detroit, Michigan, runners practice in a group called the Urban **Ninjas**. They are part of the Michigan Parkour & Freerunning Association. The larger group serves a number of functions. For example, they direct new runners to practice groups throughout the state. The association also offers tests of running skills. Those who pass the tests can then coach others.

There are countless pathways to take within any city. But the free runner has to stay mindful of what is safe and what is legal.

Open Gym

In some areas of the country, there are so many runners that leagues have formed. The Michigan group is just one example. The larger groups fill roles that smaller groups are not set up to do. In many cases, the large groups work to make sure that parks and other areas continue to welcome running. They also provide opportunities for runners from different places to get together.

Americans tend to practice free running rather than parkour, but in Europe, the opposite is true. The sports are similar, but parkour is more about being fast and efficient. Free running is more about gymnastics.

31

Plugged In

It can be difficult to run in a place where the sport has not caught on. It is especially hard to run where other people do not understand what the runner is doing. This is one reason why many people go online, looking for others who enjoy the sport. It is natural to want and to seek out the support of a group.

Any instruction that a runner gives or gets should include some safety advice.

Screen Tests

Many runners want to find people who can answer their questions. They may also feel the need to share their excitement about the sport. The Internet can be helpful with some of these issues. For example, many videos show runners doing tricks, and new runners can study them. They can read what other runners have to say about the sport. But anyone who uses the Internet also needs to follow rules of safety. They need to beware of talking to people they cannot see in person.

Beware: Some videos of free running have been edited. This can make the moves look more or less dangerous than they really are.

GETTING IT RIGHT

Sébastien Foucan has been called the father of free running. He is famous for his jumps and for the things he says about the sport. Foucan calls on runners to represent free running in a responsible way. He knows that when runners break laws or get hurt, other people want to ban the sport.

The leaders of the free running movement tell runners to stay away from alcohol and drugs. Both hurt the body and make it harder to be good at free running.

The "father of free running" encourages runners to put in as much practice as possible.

Father Knows Best

Foucan tells people to get serious training, for their good and the good of the sport. The right training helps people avoid being hurt. It also means they can show the right moves to others. Foucan wants free runners to set good examples. He tells them to be positive in their thoughts and actions, to respect other people, and to seek others who do the same. He encourages his fellow runners to build support for the sport in this way. The leaders of the free running movement have a strong antidrug message to send. Being truly strong is not possible while using drugs.

Pure Excitement

It is easy to build excitement about this sport because it is so fun to watch. Some of the moves the athletes do are hard to believe, and they attract crowds. Extreme interest in the sport has led some people to sell related items, such as T-shirts. Other people are using the athletes to help them sell products. These developments do not bother most free runners. In fact, some of them enjoy the extra attention being given to their sport. But some runners say that the changes are ruining the way things were. They liked being part of something that was not understood by most people.

Traditional sports such as regular running attract many more people because the movements are easier to make.

Free runners welcome newcomers who take the free running movement and safety seriously.

Reason to Run

As the sport becomes more popular, more runners have been able to do more to help others. Free running performers have been raising awareness of special causes. For example, one group of performers brings attention to the problem of eating disorders. Various running groups have been holding special events to raise money for causes. Many of the clubs are offering workshops to teach teens the safe way to run.

READY TO ROLL

How can you become a free runner? You can start by deciding to move like an athlete and then going outside where there is room to practice. Learn to feel the weight on your feet. Then, learn to lighten it. Start with small jumps you are sure you can complete without being hurt, and stop exercising when you feel sore. Otherwise, you may be tempted to give up before your next practice.

To build leg strength, some people train on a trampoline.

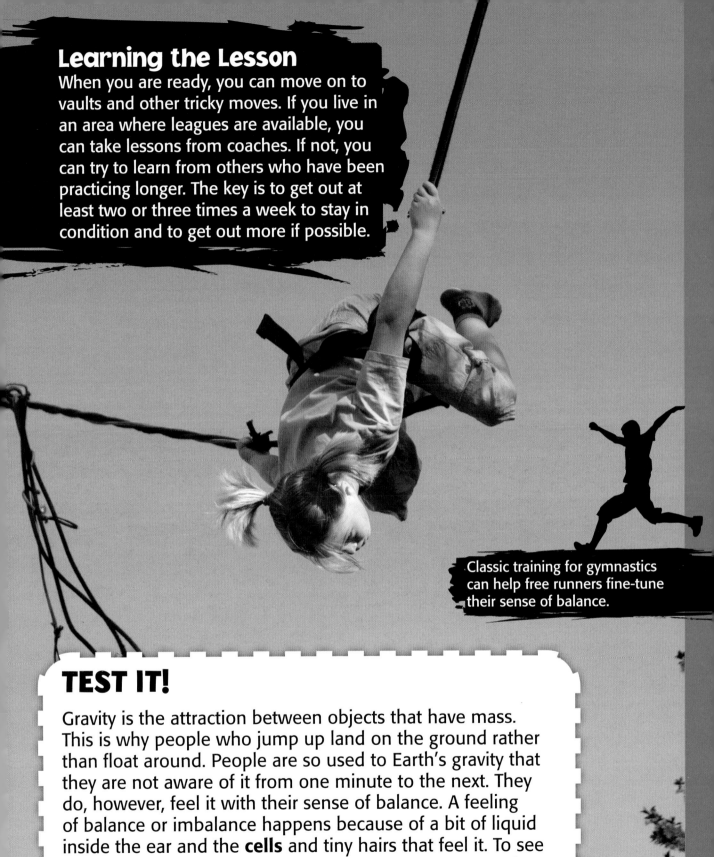

Learning the Lesson

When you are ready, you can move on to vaults and other tricky moves. If you live in an area where leagues are available, you can take lessons from coaches. If not, you can try to learn from others who have been practicing longer. The key is to get out at least two or three times a week to stay in condition and to get out more if possible.

Classic training for gymnastics can help free runners fine-tune their sense of balance.

TEST IT!

Gravity is the attraction between objects that have mass. This is why people who jump up land on the ground rather than float around. People are so used to Earth's gravity that they are not aware of it from one minute to the next. They do, however, feel it with their sense of balance. A feeling of balance or imbalance happens because of a bit of liquid inside the ear and the **cells** and tiny hairs that feel it. To see how the ear helps you sense gravity, try spinning around quickly a few times. Do you feel a change in your sense of balance?

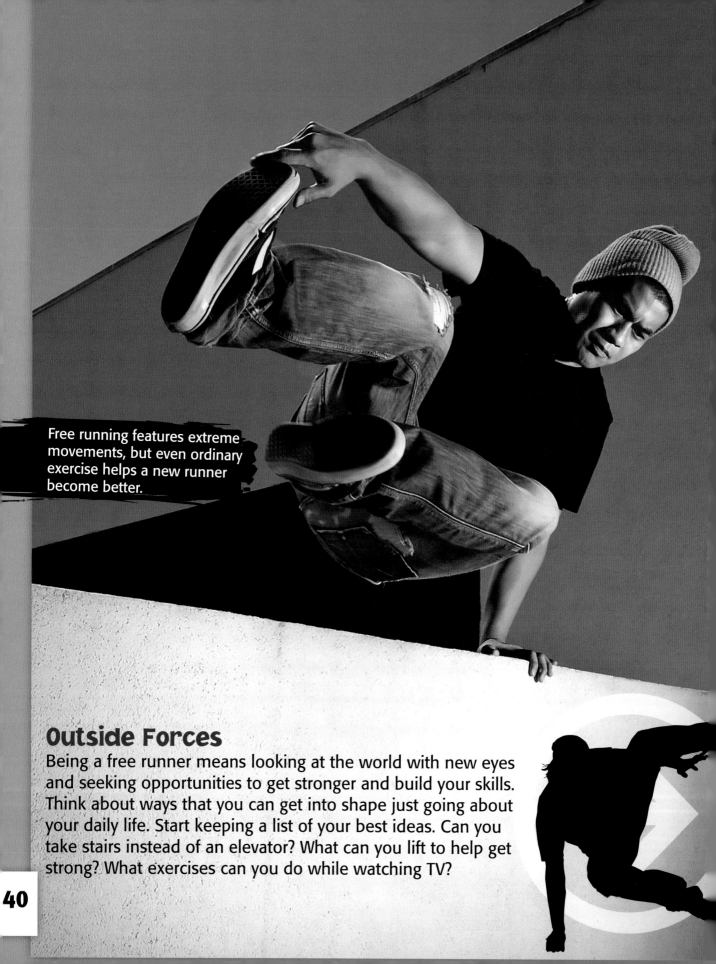

Free running features extreme movements, but even ordinary exercise helps a new runner become better.

Outside Forces

Being a free runner means looking at the world with new eyes and seeking opportunities to get stronger and build your skills. Think about ways that you can get into shape just going about your daily life. Start keeping a list of your best ideas. Can you take stairs instead of an elevator? What can you lift to help get strong? What exercises can you do while watching TV?

A Running Start

Free runners around the country and across the world will be practicing the sport today. To get started, you do not need to wait another day, either. There is no need to spend a lot of money or do much more than get permission to go where you need to go. Running shoes are sold at yard sales and in resale shops. Most towns have a park, and most parks are less crowded at certain times of day. Doing push-ups is as simple as dropping to the floor, and eating right is a choice you can make, starting now.

Strength comes from being strong.

The classic moves of free running need to be learned the old-fashioned way — through lots of practice.

FEET FIRST

In free running, the word *tricking* means performing a stunt. Many of the special terms used in this sport describe the kinds of tricks that runners do. A *gap jump*, for example, is a jump over a gap. A *tic tac* is pushing off one thing with your foot in order to turn around and aim higher at something else. To *muscle-up* is to move from a hanging position to a spot above an object, using the arms.

Words for It

Free running stunts borrow much of their style from the martial arts. The *parkour roll*, for example, is similar to the kind of roll seen in martial arts movies. The runner tucks in his or her body and rolls shoulder first.

Words in Context

Can you guess the meaning of these free running words and phrases?

1. He did that *monkey vault* like he's been doing that every day. He's like Kong.

   monkey vault: passing over an object with hands on the object and legs between the arms

2. I have been doing that *wall run* so often, I could run it with my eyes closed.

   wall run: a run along the top of a wall

3. No need to show off when a *lazy vault* will get you there.

   lazy vault: when legs pass over an object first and hand or hands barely touch the object

LEGENDS OF FREE RUNNING

The legends of free running are men and women whose skills and daring stand out. Some have been pioneers of the sport, and others have been bringing attention to the sport through their work in movies.

Five Famous Free Runners

David Belle is famous for his ability to jump from one building to another. In 2004, he starred in a movie called *Banlieue 13*, which cemented his reputation as the founder of parkour.

Sébastien Foucan is thought of as the founder of free running. His reputation grew after the stunts he performed in the 2006 James Bond movie *Casino Royale*.

MTV aired a show called *Ultimate Parkour Challenge* for the first time in 2009, and on that first season **Daniel Ilabaca** won the $10,000 prize.

According to Guinness World Records, the record for most circular jumps on a wall is 11. This feat was achieved by American **Aung Zaw Oo** in 2010.

The record for most forward roll front flips in one minute is 17. This record was set by **Mathew Kaye**, of Great Britain, in 2010.

Behind the Legends

The Yamakasi, of France, is a well-known group of parkour performers. *Yamakasi* means "strong body" or "strong spirit" in a language spoken in Africa. The group practiced together in the 1990s and made a movie in 2001, which made them famous. Five of the original members now work together in a production business called Parkour Generations.

name	position at Parkour Generations
Châu Belle Dinh	arranges stunts and performances for films and major events
Guylain N'Guba Boyeke	plans and arranges moves for group performances
Laurent Piemontesi	works as senior coach and instructor and also as an author
Williams Belle	youngest member, works as a performer and consultant
Yann H'Nautra	teaches world-famous Cirque du Soleil and other performers

Ready, Action!

The obstacles to becoming an expert in this sport's history are few. You can use your library, and the Internet, to learn more about free running and parkour. Here are some key terms and names that you might want to research.

Yamakasi	3RUN
art of movement	The Tribe
Les Traceurs	Tempest
Jump London	Chase Armitage
Prince of Persia	Raymond Belle
District 13	Tim Shieff

Glossary

cells: the smallest basic part of a living thing

freestyle: allowing any trick or move from a somewhat standard set of tricks or moves

gravity: attraction between objects that have mass

gymnastics: exercises that build body strength and coordination

hydrated: supported with enough water for health

indigenous: native; natural to or originating from a particular place

martial arts: any of several forms of fighting that are practiced as a sport

mass: measure of the amount of material something contains

momentum: the force of a moving object

ninjas: people who use martial arts and stealth

obstacle: of or relating to a thing that is in the way; also, a thing in the way

protein: compound in plant and animal materials that is needed for animal growth

scale: to climb up

stamina: staying power

urban: of or relating to a city

vault: a leap made with the help of the hands

vertical: upright; running up and down

For More Information

Books

Bloom, Marc. *Young Runners: The Complete Guide to Healthy Running for Kids from 5 to 18.* New York, NY: Simon & Schuster, 2009.

Challen, Paul. *Flip It Gymnastics.* New York, NY: Crabtree, 2010.

Goodrow, Carol. *Kids Running: Have Fun, Get Faster & Go Farther.* Halcottsville, NY: Breakaway Books, 2008.

Iedwab, Claudio, and Roxanne Standefer. *The Peaceful Way: A Children's Guide to the Traditions of the Martial Arts.* Rochester, VT: Destiny Books, 2001.

For Mature or Guided Readers

Foucan, Sébastien. *Freerunning: Find Your Way.* London, UK: Michael O'Mara Books, 2009.

Websites

American Parkour
www.americanparkour.com/
American Parkour is an website created by professional runners. The videos on the site show their moves and accomplishments Please be warned: The moves portrayed have been made by practiced professionals.

Parkour Generations
www.parkourgenerations.com/
This website highlights the activities and accomplishments of a famous group of parkour professionals.

Publisher's note to educators and parents: Our editors have carefully reviewed these websites to ensure that they are suitable for students. Many websites change frequently, however, and we cannot guarantee that a site's future contents will continue to meet our high standards of quality and educational value. Be advised that students should be closely supervised whenever they access the Internet.

Index

balanced 9
Belle, David 13, 44, 45
benches 5, 24
Bond, James 13, 44

cartwheels 27
Casino Royale 13, 44
cells 39
chin-ups 25
clothing 23
club 26
competition 28
condition 39
crunches 25

drills 27

Foucan, Sébastien 34, 35, 44, 47
freestyle 4, 13

goals 29
gravity 7, 39
gymnastics 5, 31, 39

handstands 29
Hébert, Georges 14, 15
hydrated 24

Ilabaca, Daniel 44
injury 6, 9
Internet 33, 45

Kaye, Mathew 44
Keaton, Buster 13

martial arts 12, 42
mass 7, 39
momentum 15

ninjas 15, 30

obstacle 10, 14, 15, 22, 23, 24, 45
Olympics 13
Oo, Aung Zaw 44

parkour 4, 12, 13, 14, 30, 31, 42, 44,
        45, 47
permission 26, 29, 41
physical education 14
pledges 37
protein 25
push-ups 41

railings 4, 24
respect 11, 35

shoes 6, 22, 23, 41
stairway 4
stamina 25
stunts 4, 12, 13, 42, 44

urban 18, 30

vault 4, 24, 39, 43
vertical 9
videos 13, 33, 47